Railway Series No. 2

THOMAS, THE TANK ENGINE

by

THE REV. W. AWDRY

HEINEMANN · LONDON

William Heinemann Ltd
Michelin House
81 Fulham Road
London SW3 6RB

LONDON   MELBOURNE   AUCKLAND

First published in 1946
Copyright © William Heinemann Ltd 1946
Reprinted 1991
All rights reserved

ISBN 0 434 92779 1

Printed and bound in Great Britain by
William Clowes Limited, Beccles and London

DEAR CHRISTOPHER,

Here is your friend Thomas, the Tank Engine. He wanted to come out of his station-yard and see the world. These stories tell you how he did it.

I hope you will like them because you helped me to make them.

YOUR LOVING DADDY

Thomas and Gordon

THOMAS was a tank engine who lived at a Big Station. He had six small wheels, a short stumpy funnel, a short stumpy boiler, and a short stumpy dome.

He was a fussy little engine, always pulling coaches about. He pulled them to the station ready for the big engines to take out on long journeys; and when trains came in, and the people had got out, he would pull the empty coaches away, so that the big engines could go and rest.

He was a cheeky little engine, too. He thought no engine worked as hard as he did. So he used to play tricks on them. He liked best of all to come quietly beside a big engine dozing on a siding and make him jump.

"Peep, peep, peep, pip, peep! Wake up, lazibones!" he would whistle, "why don't you work hard like me?"

Then he would laugh rudely and run away to find some more coaches.

One day Gordon was resting on a siding. He was very tired. The big express he always pulled had been late, and he had had to run as fast as he could to make up for lost time.

He was just going to sleep when Thomas came up in his cheeky way.

"Wake up, lazibones," he whistled, "do some hard work for a change—you can't catch me!" and he ran off laughing.

Instead of going to sleep again, Gordon thought how he could pay Thomas out.

One morning Thomas wouldn't wake up. His driver and fireman couldn't make him start. His fire went out and there was not enough steam.

It was nearly time for the express. The people were waiting, but the coaches weren't ready.

At last Thomas started. "Oh, dear! Oh, dear!" he yawned.

"Come on," said the coaches. "Hurry up." Thomas gave them a rude bump, and started for the station.

"Don't stop dawdling, don't stop dawdling," he grumbled.

"Where have you been? Where have you been?" asked the coaches crossly.

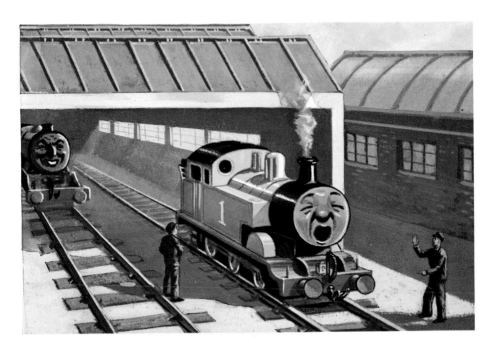

Thomas fussed into the station where Gordon was waiting.

"Poop, poop, poop. Hurry up, you," said Gordon crossly.

"Peep, pip, peep. Hurry yourself," said cheeky Thomas.

"Yes," said Gordon, "I will," and almost before the coaches had stopped moving Gordon came out of his siding and was coupled to the train.

"Poop, poop," he whistled. "Get in quickly, please." So the people got in quickly, the signal went down, the clock struck the hour, the guard waved his green flag, and Gordon was ready to start.

Thomas usually pushed behind the big trains to help them start. But he was always uncoupled first, so that when the train was running nicely he could stop and go back.

This time he was late, and Gordon started so quickly that they forgot to uncouple Thomas.

"Poop, poop," said Gordon.

"Peep, peep, peep," whistled Thomas.

"Come on! Come on!" puffed Gordon to the coaches.

"Pull harder! Pull harder!" puffed Thomas to Gordon.

The heavy train slowly began to move out of the station.

The train went faster and faster; too fast for Thomas. He wanted to stop but he couldn't.

"Peep! peep! stop! stop!" he whistled.

"Hurry, hurry, hurry," laughed Gordon in front.

"You can't get away. You can't get away," laughed the coaches.

Poor Thomas was going faster than he had ever gone before. He was out of breath, and his wheels hurt him, but he had to go on.

"I shall never be the same again," he thought sadly, "My wheels will be quite worn out."

At last they stopped at a station. Everyone laughed to see Thomas puffing and panting behind.

They uncoupled him, put him on to a turn-table and then he ran on a siding out of the way.

"Well, little Thomas," chuckled Gordon as he passed, "now you know what hard work means, don't you?"

Poor Thomas couldn't answer, he had no breath. He just puffed slowly away to rest, and had a long, long drink.

He went home very slowly, and was careful afterwards never to be cheeky to Gordon again.

Thomas's Train

THOMAS often grumbled because he was not allowed to pull passenger trains.

The other engines laughed. "You're too impatient," they said. "You'd be sure to leave something behind!"

"Rubbish," said Thomas, crossly. "You just wait, I'll show you."

One night he and Henry were alone. Henry was ill. The men worked hard, but he didn't get better.

Now Henry usually pulled the first train in the morning, and Thomas had to get his coaches ready.

"If Henry is ill," he thought, "perhaps I shall pull his train."

Thomas ran to find the coaches.

"Come *along*. Come *along*," he fussed.

"There's plenty of time, there's plenty of time," grumbled the coaches.

He took them to the platform, and wanted to run round in front at once. But his driver wouldn't let him.

"Don't be impatient, Thomas," he said.

So Thomas waited and waited. The people got in, the guard and stationmaster walked up and down, the porters banged the doors, and still Henry didn't come.

Thomas got more and more excited every minute.

The fat director came out of his office to see what was the matter, and the guard and the stationmaster told him about Henry.

"Find another engine," he ordered.

"There's only Thomas," they said.

"You'll have to do it then, Thomas. Be quick now!"

So Thomas ran round to the front and backed down on the coaches ready to start.

"Don't be impatient," said his driver. "Wait till everything is ready."

But Thomas was too excited to listen to a word he said.

What happened then no one knows. Perhaps they forgot to couple Thomas to the train; perhaps Thomas was too impatient to wait till they were ready; or perhaps his driver pulled the lever by mistake.

Anyhow, Thomas started. People shouted and waved at him but he didn't stop.

"They're waving because I'm such a splendid engine," he thought importantly. "Henry says it's hard to pull trains, but *I* think it's easy."

"Hurry! hurry! hurry!" he puffed, pretending to be like Gordon.

As he passed the first signal-box, he saw the men leaning out waving and shouting.

"They're pleased to see me," he thought. "They've never seen *me* pulling a train before—it's nice of them to wave," and he whistled, "Peep, peep, thank you," and hurried on.

But he came to a signal at "Danger."

"Bother!" he thought. "I must stop, and I was going so nicely, too. What a nuisance signals are!" And he blew an angry "Peep, peep" on his whistle.

One of the signalmen ran up. "Hullo, Thomas!" he said. "What are you doing here?"

"I'm pulling a train," said Thomas proudly. "Can't you *see*?"

"Where are your coaches, then?"

Thomas looked back. "Why bless me," he said, "if we haven't left them behind!"

"Yes," said the signalman, "you'd better go back quickly and fetch them."

Poor Thomas was so sad he nearly cried.

"Cheer up!" said his driver. "Let's go back quickly, and try again."

At the station all the passengers were talking at once. They were telling the fat director, the stationmaster and the guard what a bad railway it was.

But when Thomas came back and they saw how sad he was, they couldn't be cross. So they coupled him to the train, and this time he *really* pulled it.

But for a long time afterwards the other engines laughed at Thomas, and said:

"Look, there's Thomas, who wanted to pull a train, but forgot about the coaches!"

Thomas and the Trucks

THOMAS used to grumble in the shed at night.

"I'm tired of pushing coaches, I want to see the world."

The others didn't take much notice, for Thomas was a little engine with a long tongue.

But one night, Edward came to the shed. He was a kind little engine, and felt sorry for Thomas.

"I've got some trucks to take home tomorrow," he told him. "If you take them instead, I'll push coaches in the yard."

"Thank you," said Thomas, "that will be nice."

So they asked their drivers next morning, and when they said "Yes," Thomas ran happily to find the trucks.

Now trucks are silly and noisy. They talk a lot and don't attend to what they are doing. They don't listen to their engine, and when he stops they bump into each other screaming.

"Oh! Oh! Oh! Oh! Whatever is happening?"

And, I'm sorry to say, they play tricks on an engine who is not used to them.

Edward knew all about trucks. He warned
Thomas to be careful, but Thomas was too
excited to listen.

The shunter fastened the coupling, and, when
the signal dropped, Thomas was ready.

The guard blew his whistle. "Peep! peep!"
answered Thomas and started off.

But the trucks weren't ready.

"Oh! Oh! Oh! Oh!" they screamed as their
couplings tightened. "Wait, Thomas, wait."
But Thomas wouldn't wait.

"Come—on; come—on," he puffed, and
the trucks grumbled slowly out of the siding on
to the main line.

Thomas was happy. "Come along. Come along," he puffed.

"All—right! — don't — fuss — all — right! —don't fuss," grumbled the trucks. They clattered through stations, and rumbled over bridges.

Thomas whistled "Peep! peep!" and they rushed through the tunnel in which Henry had been shut up.

Then they came to the top of the hill where Gordon had stuck.

"Steady now, steady," warned the driver, and he shut off steam, and began to put on the brakes.

"We're stopping, we're stopping," called Thomas.

"No! No! No! No!" answered the trucks, and bumped into each other. "Go — on! — go — on!" and before his driver could stop them, they had pushed Thomas down the hill, and were rattling and laughing behind him.

Poor Thomas tried hard to stop them from making him go too fast.

"Stop pushing, stop pushing," he hissed, but the trucks would not stop.

"Go — on! — go — on!" they giggled in their silly way.

He was glad when they got to the bottom. Then he saw in front the place where they had to stop.

"Oh, dear! What shall I do?"

They rattled through the station, and luckily the line was clear as they swerved into the goods yard.

"Oo — — — — — — ooh e — — — — —r," groaned Thomas, as his brakes held fast and he skidded along the rails.

"I must stop," and he shut his eyes tight.

When he opened them he saw he had stopped just in front of the buffers, and there watching him was ———

The fat director!

"What are *you* doing here, Thomas?" he asked sternly.

"I've brought Edward's trucks," Thomas answered.

"Why did you come so fast?"

"I didn't mean to, I was *pushed*," said Thomas sadly.

"Haven't you pulled trucks before?"

"No."

"Then you've a lot to learn about trucks, little Thomas. They are silly things and must be kept in their place. After pushing them about here for a few weeks you'll know almost as much about them as Edward. Then you'll be a Really Useful Engine."

Thomas and the Breakdown Train

EVERY day the fat director came to the station to catch his train, and he always said "Hullo" to Thomas.

There were lots of trucks in the yard— different ones came in every day—and Thomas had to push and pull them into their right places.

He worked hard—he knew now that he wasn't so clever as he had thought. Besides, the fat director had been kind to him and he wanted to learn all about trucks so as to be a Really Useful Engine.

But on a siding by themselves were some trucks that Thomas was told he "mustn't touch."

There was a small coach, some flat trucks, and two queer things his driver called cranes.

"That's the breakdown train," he said. "When there's an accident, the workmen get into the coach, and the engine takes them quickly to help the hurt people, and to clear and mend the line. The cranes are for lifting heavy things like engines, and coaches, and trucks."

One day, Thomas was in the yard, when he heard an engine whistling "Help! Help!" and a goods train came rushing through much too fast.

The engine (a new one called James) was frightened. His brake blocks were on fire, and smoke and sparks streamed out on each side.

"They're *pushing* me! They're *pushing* me!" he panted.

"On! On! On! On!" laughed the trucks; and still whistling "Help! Help!" poor James disappeared under a bridge.

"I'd like to teach those trucks a lesson," said Thomas the Tank Engine.

Presently a bell rang in the signal-box, and a man came running, "James is off the line—the breakdown train—quickly," he shouted.

So Thomas was coupled on, the workmen jumped into their coach, and off they went.

Thomas worked his hardest. "Hurry! Hurry! Hurry!" he puffed, and this time he wasn't pretending to be like Gordon, he really meant it.

"Bother those trucks and their tricks," he thought, "I hope poor James isn't hurt."

They found James and the trucks at a bend in the line. The brake-van and the last few trucks were on the rails, but the front ones were piled in a heap; James was in a field with a cow looking at him, and his driver and fireman were feeling him all over to see if he was hurt.

"Never mind, James," they said. "It wasn't your fault, it was those wooden brakes they gave you. We always said they were no good."

Thomas pushed the breakdown train alongside. Then he pulled the unhurt trucks out of the way.

"Oh —— dear! — oh — dear!" they groaned.

"Serves you right. Serves you right," puffed Thomas crossly.

When the men put other trucks on the line he pulled them away, too. He was hard at work puffing backwards and forwards all the afternoon.

"This'll teach you a lesson, this'll teach you a lesson," he told the trucks, and they answered "Yes — it — will — yes — it — will," in a sad, groany, creaky, sort of voice.

They left the broken trucks and mended the line. Then with two cranes they put James back on the rails. He tried to move but he couldn't, so Thomas helped him back to the shed.

The fat director was waiting anxiously for them.

"Well, Thomas," he said kindly, "I've heard all about it, and I'm very pleased with you. You're a Really Useful Engine.

"James shall have some proper brakes and a new coat of paint, and you ——————— shall have a Branch Line all to yourself."

"Oh, sir!" said Thomas, happily.

Now Thomas is as happy as can be. He has a branch line all to himself, and puffs proudly backwards and forwards with two coaches all day.

He is never lonely, because there is always some engine to talk to at the junction.

Edward and Henry stop quite often, and tell him the news. Gordon is always in a hurry and does not stop; but he never forgets to say "Poop, poop" to little Thomas, and Thomas always whistles "Peep, peep" in return.